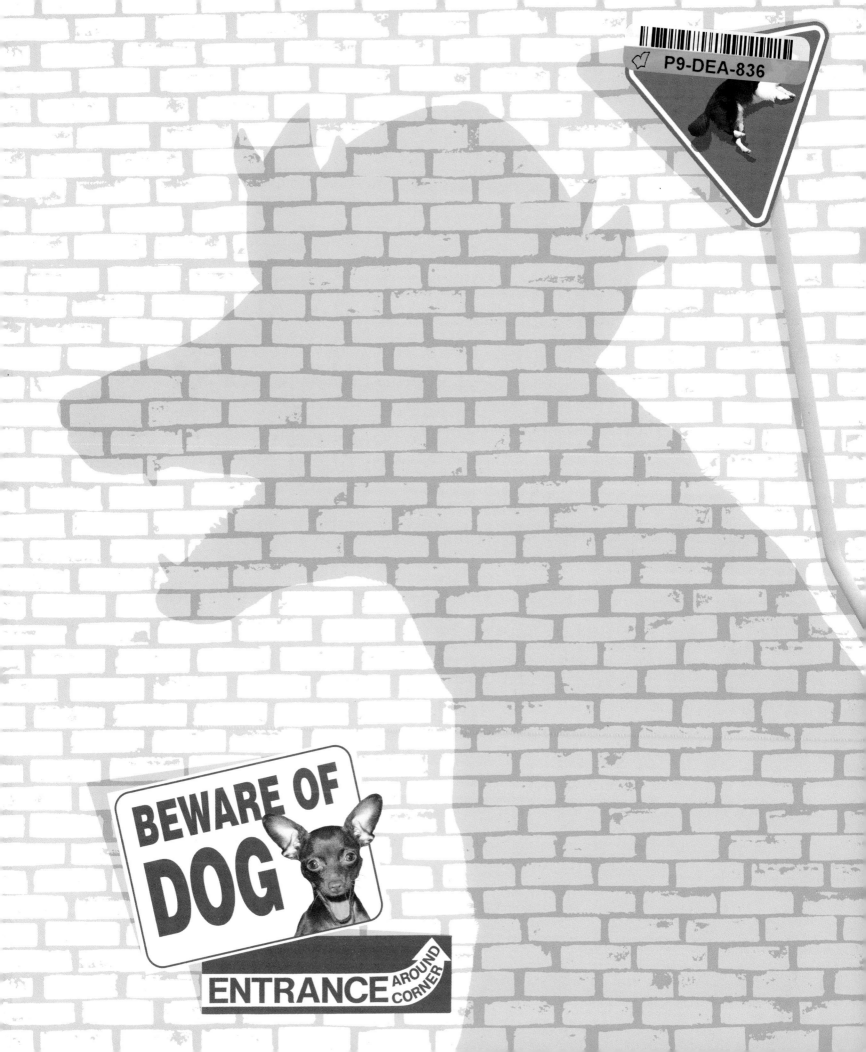

It was just one of those days. Nothing was **hunky-dory** for good, old **HUNKY-DORY**. With a hope and a sigh, he flipped open the newspaper, searching for a job.

With a CRINKLE-CRUNKLE-RUSTLE of noisy newspapers, the whole WORLD read this ad:

WANTED

FIERCE, SNARLING GUARD DOGS

CAN'T SLEEP? COUNT SHEEP!

Protect those ewes, rams, and little lambs. A growl a day keeps the wolves away. Don't pull the wool over your eyes, this is a great job. Call 123—BAAAAAAAAAAA

Howls of fun!

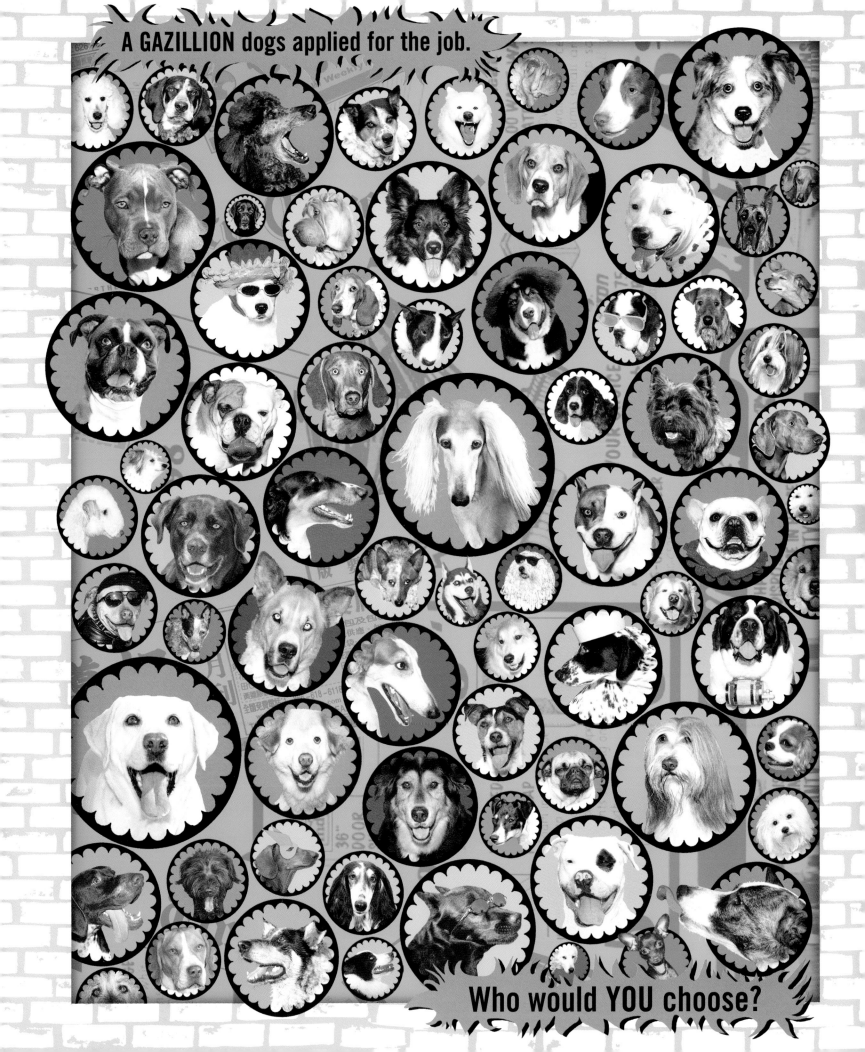

A GAZILLION dogs applied for the job.

Who would YOU choose?

These dogs were **apPAWled** when they **didn't** get the job.

But these dogs were **PAWsitively delighted**
because they **DID** get the job!

They packed their bags
and headed for the hills.

USUAL ROUTE

Henny-Penny
RESTAURANT

Great!
FOOD

MRS. MUSTARD'S EXPRESS

NEVER CRY WOOF!

HOWLED AND GROWLED BY

JANE WATTENBERG

DOGGEDLY
PHOTOGRAPHED
BY HER, TOO!

A Dog-U-Drama

SCHOLASTIC PRESS
NEW YORK

The **SHEEPBURBS**

BIX was eager.
"I can't wait 'til I see a **wolf!**
Bring 'em on! They don't
scare me. Only **wet paint**
would **run.**"

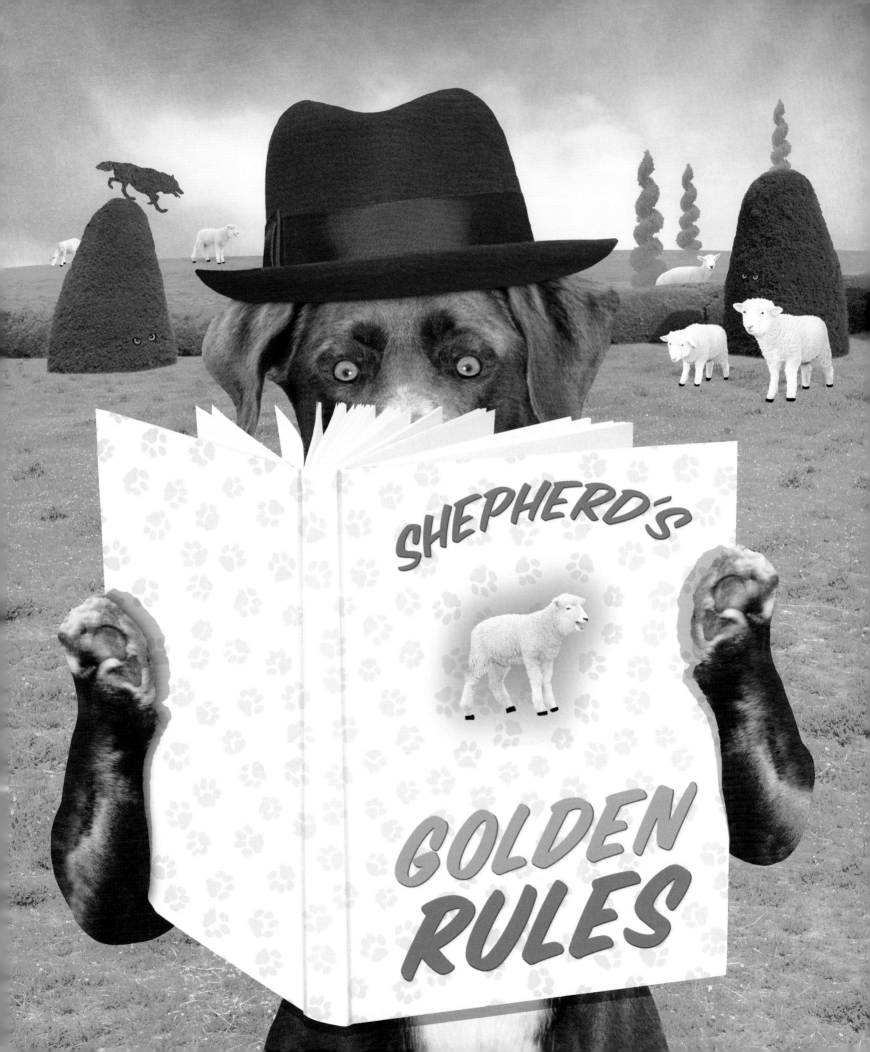

But HUNKY-DORY was cautious.
"Now remember the rules."

"O, blithering **bother!**"
moaned BIX.

"The sun is so **hot**,"
groaned BIX.

"I'm crushingly **lonely**,"
phoned BIX.

He knew he **shouldn't.**
He thought he **wouldn't.**
But what's a lone dog to do?

BIX let loose
an electrifying,
spine-tingling,
hair-punking,
"**WOOOO**

OOF!"

DOUBLE CROSSING

Meanwhile, over on yonder hills **ears quivered.**

What's that?

BIX howling?
Wolves prowling?

Knowing just what to do,
HUNKY-DORY roared,
"ALL DOGS TO THE RESCUE!"

When they arrived, there sat BIX,

grinning big.

"**What's the story?**" asked HUNKY-DORY.

"Aw, nothing's at the pump, chump,"
swaggered BIX. "Relax a bit.
I crave your company.
It's so hard talking to these rams.
They keep **BUTTING** in!"

"BIX, we've left our sheep
to rescue you and **there's
not a wolf in sight.**
Bother us for a **reason**
next season," grumbled
HUNKY-DORY.

Miffed, they **rushed**
back to their **sheep.**

But BIX
couldn't stand it.

"There's nada, **nothing, zip** to DO out here in this **ding**-dang-**dong**-dell.

Watching fluffballs 24–7 is **not** the cat's pajamas.

It's *PARTY* time. **Catch this:**

WOOO OOOF!"

"Lying again? You fungus! You garlic! You wormwood! You skunk! Just you wait for a **real wolf** to nibble your **knobby nose,**" warned HUNKY-DORY.

"Aw, HUNK-A-DUNK, that will **never** happen to a **happening hound** like **me.**"

Mopey and blue, feeling like glue, BIX called to his flock,

"Hey fluffballs! Ewe-ram-a-lamb-a-ding-dongs!

Wanna play HIDE-AND-PEEK?"

GOOSE CT
GOOSE RD

BIX began counting: "1, 6, 2, 9, 44, 3 . . ."
and just as the words, "Ready or not, here I come"
dripped off his tongue, he found himself
nose to nose with . . .

. . . a WOLF!

"Hogwash!" spat HUNKY-DORY.
"Who would believe that mutt?
Twice wasn't nice, but a third is absurd."

NO ONE MOVED A PAW.

TRUTH OR CONSEQUENCES
just down the road

"Oh, woe!
WHAT NOW?" wailed BIX.
"I guess it's swim or sink.
Even skunks make a stink.
So let me at 'em!"

Ka-ping!

Ka-pow!

But **FLEAS LOUISE!**
What's a **lone dog** to do
when he has a **hunch**
he's **lunch?**

Get UP and *R U N !*

WHEEZY and QUEASY, BIX howled,
"Look out, HUNK-A-CHUNK, wolves are everywhere!
They're devouring my sheep and almost
ate me up, too! You've got to help!"

"Oh sure, Braveheart. Good story," muttered HUNKY-DORY. "Those wolves would never eat you, BIX. Wolves don't eat clowns . . . they taste funny!"

They laughed and whooped and laughed some more, and *everything* was hunky-dory . . .

. . . or was it?

SEE
EWE

ABOUT THIS BOOK

Never Cry WOOF! is an adaptation of Aesop's fable *The Boy Who Cried Wolf*, also known as *The Shepherd Boy and the Wolf*. It is thought that Aesop lived in ancient Greece around 600 B.C., first as a slave, later as a famous sage and ambassador for a king. Never tarnished by time, Aesop's stories still shine with meaning and shake our world today.

BEST OF SHOW

• • • All animals in this book were happy to be photographed • • •

Steve Sultan (BIX), Sancho Panza Frink (HUNKY-DORY), Bandit Reed, Quinn and Julian Forsythe, Rascal Sozzi, Bandit and Tobey Vaugn Hock, Nelly Sonneborn-Greenberg, Rex Wong-Sanchez, Toby Houston-Hamilton, Salsa Gordon-Talbot, Twiggy Cawley, Sophie Marcus, Sir Edward the Hopeful Caldwell, Ajax Gavin-Loughlin, Paco Forootan, Kayla Merryman, Bear Reed, Charlie Selkowitz, Penny Cruciger, Elvie Caputo, Dee-Dee Taylor Sultan, Duke Hoenigman, Nora Destino, Cassidy Bush, Buddy Rutzen, Jazzy Watson, Cha-Cha Munoz-Lake, Odessa Thompson, Freddy Dyadko, Oliver Lumsden, Baby Tanaka, Figaro Lieberman, Popeye La Pu Patrick, Felix Wright, Ted Salwen, Cody Stewart-Knight, Ashley Maulis, Woody and Darwin Lynch, Cowboy Richheimer-Lindner, Holly Van Tress, Travis Sternbach, Moxie Wattenberg-Chase, and assorted mystery dogs. • Working mule of Palena, Italy • Romney sheep from www.TawandaFarms.com • And the wily wolves: Neawa, Sioban, and Darwin from Cougar Hill Ranch, Monty and Kena Borgna

A WORLD OF THANKS

Tracy Snelling, Julia Frink of Dogwalks.com, Kelly and Larry Sultan, Tricia and Foster Reed, Carol Pasheilich and Maggie Howard, Laura Burges and the exuberant third-grade class at The San Francisco School, Lisa Fruchtman, Sasha Wizansky, Patrick Niesten, Georgia Hammerich, Marina Marino, and Gianni di Vincenzo.

OUT OF THIS WORLD THANKS

Tracy Mack, David Saylor, and Leslie Budnick, incomparable editorial dream team. Kendra Marcus, super-agent and friend. Gideon Chase, astute reviewer of the dailies. Samuel, sage luminary, light of my life. And remembering Grandpa Sam Daven with his hunky-dory hat.